Frederick the fox

Written and Illustrated by
Kaitlin E. Carlson

Frederick the Fox Series – Book 1
First paperback edition
Independently Published

Book design by Kaitlin E. Carlson
Illustrations by Kaitlin E. Carlson
Jacket Photograph by Tanya De of Tanya De Photography

ISBN (paperback): 9781794319585

frederickfoxbooks@gmail.com

FOR JOSEPHINE, AARON, AMELIA, AND LOUISE,
YOU FILL MY WORLD WITH SO MUCH HAPPY

Frederick

is a small.

very shy. red fox.

He has white socks

on his feet.

fluffy white fur

on his chest.

and his ears are

white

and

pointed.

His home is a tree

        in the woods.

frederick lives

        all by himself

                in a cozy foxhole.

There are other foxes

        that live nearby.

    but frederick is too shy to talk to them.

One sunny.

spring day

frederick was

running

through

his favorite

field of tulips

when he heard a

small.

sad

sound

coming from

one of the

flowers.

frederick didn't

stop because

he didn't like

talking to

new

people.

But as he ran through the field,

frederick decided

to stop

and see where

the sound was

coming from.

He peeked over

the edge of a large.

yellow

tulip

and a tiny. shaking

field mouse

with huge eyes

let out a

startled
and
terrified

squeak.

"I didn't mean to startle you"

frederick said shyly.

"My name is frederick.
What is yours?"

"M-M-Maisie" the small mouse squeaked.

"Why are you crying, Maisie?"

frederick asked quietly.

Between tiny sniffles,

Maisie answered.

"I live on the

other side of this

field and the rain

last night flooded my home.

I walked as far

as I could and

fell asleep in this flower."

Frederick didn't know

how to help Maisie

with her flooded home.

"I'm sorry you've

lost your home"

frederick said

with a

small
voice

as he turned to leave.

He was too shy

to say

anything else.

As frederick continued
through the tulips.
he thought about

his warm

and

cozy foxhole.

"I'm sure there is
enough room in my home
to share with a

small

field

mouse."
he thought to himself.

Turning around. he quickly ran
back to Maisie.

"Maisie" frederick said.

"I have a very

warm, dry foxhole.

Would you like to

share it with me until

you find a new home?"

Maisie's big
              eyes got
                            even bigger.

                    "No.
                    No.
        I don't think that's a good idea."
            She said very quickly.

Maisie had always
                been told that
                            foxes eat field mice.

"That's okay.

Goodbye, Maisie"

frederick said,

feeling
embarrassed.

Unsure of what else to say,
frederick turned
around to leave.

Maisie was not
sure what to do.
frederick seemed like
a
nice
fox.

He had stopped
to make sure
she was okay,
and he hadn't
even tried
to eat her!

"Okay!" Maisie shouted. "I'll go with you."

frederick happily ran back to Maisie and crouched down to let Maisie jump on his back. "You can hold onto my fur and I'll carry you" frederick offered.

Tentatively. Maisie stepped off the flower and onto frederick's back. "Hold on!" frederick shouted. as he turned and ran back to his foxhole.

At the edge of the woods Maisie heard a soft hooting. frederick stopped underneath a tall, very old tree.

"Whooo do you have there, frederick?" A wise, old owl asked.

"This is Maisie. Her home was flooded last night. She's going to live in the forest with us."

Orwin, the owl quietly hooted.

"Welcome to the forest, Maisie."

Frederick and Maisie
continued
through the forest.

Soon, they came
across a family
of bluebirds.

A small, baby
peeked out from
under her mom's wings

and happily
chirped at
Maisie.

Leaping over logs
and ducking
under branches.
Maisie held on tightly
as frederick continued
through the forest.
Maisie glanced to
the side and let out
a small squeak of surprise.

There was a
small doe running
next to them!
frederick glanced
to the side.
"Don't worry. Maisie."
he said "that's Darla.
She lives in
the forest too.
and loves to run.
She's very shy
and won't come
too close."

Slowing to a walk.
frederick glanced
side-to-side.
and stopped
at the edge of
a small clearing.
Maisie noticed
a chattering sound
high up in the trees
that was getting closer.
looking around.
Maisie saw that the
branches were full of squirrels.

frederick walked to
the other side
of the clearing
while Maisie
looked at the
woods around her.

She noticed many
pairs of eyes
looking at her
from behind the trees.
"We're here!"
frederick said brightly.

Maisie thought
the foxhole
looked very small.
Hardly enough
room for a
fox and a mouse.

Maisie hopped

down and scurried

up to the tree.

She peeked

inside and

was so surprised!

frederick's home

was very large

on the inside.

"Maisie.

I'm going to go

tell the other foxes

that you're here.

I'll be right back."

frederick said

as he turned

and hurried

through the trees.

"No!"

a bigger, older fox told frederick.

"A field mouse cannot live here with us."

frederick didn't understand why the other foxes didn't want Maisie to live with them in the forest.

"She's not like us. frederick. She would be better off living by herself" another fox said.

"Or with another mouse family!" another fox shouted.

Maisie could hear
the foxes grumbling.
Quietly, she walked
towards them,
hiding behind trees.
When she heard
how angry the
other foxes were
she felt afraid.
Maisie started
running through
the forest,
back to where
her old home
used to be.

As frederick walked
back to his home.
he felt very sad
that the other foxes
didn't want Maisie
to live in the
forest with them.
He didn't want to
tell her that
she had to leave.
Suddenly, frederick
turned around
and ran back
to the group of foxes.
"No!" he shouted.

Startled. the foxes
all turned and
looked at him.

"Maisie has no home
and we have all of
this forest to share.

Imagine if we lost our
homes and had
nowhere to sleep".

frederick continued.
"Imagine if I was
in a strange place

with no place to sleep".
The foxes started
whispering to each other.

"you're right, frederick"

the big,
old
fox said.

"We have all of this

forest to share.

Maisie should

stay with us."

Happy that the foxes

changed their minds.

frederick ran back

to
his
foxhole.

When he got there

Maisie was nowhere

to be found.

"Maisie?" frederick said.

searching
the
woods

around their home.

"Maisie" he said

again

louder.

He turned towards

the path out

of the forest.

"Maisie!" he shouted.

Worried that Maisie
might be hurt or lost.
frederick started
running through
the forest
shouting her name.

He quickly ran
past the squirrels
askeing if they
had seen her.
"We saw her
running that way."
they said. pointing
toward the path
out of the forest.

When Maisie got to the
                    edge of the forest
                              she could hear footsteps
coming towards her.
                    She moved behind
                              a tree so no one
could see her.
                    but frederick saw her
                              before she disappeared.
"Maisie! Wait!"
                    frederick said with relief.
                              "Where are you going?"
"frederick" Maisie said.
                    "I heard what the
                              other foxes said.
I'm going to
          find somewhere
                    else to live."

"Oh no!" frederick said.
"I talked to
the other foxes.
I asked how they
would feel if
they didn't have a home.
They changed
their minds. Maisie!
your home is with us.
you can live with
the owls. and bluebirds.
and deer.
and squirrels.
and foxes."

"Oh. frederick"

said Maisie

"I don't know.

What if they

change their minds?"

"You're my friend. Maisie.

You're welcome

in the forest

and you're welcome

in my home." he said.

"Okay!"

Maisie said happily.

She scurried onto

frederick's back

as he turned around

to

go

home.

At the edge

of the forest

Maisie heard the

wise, old owl saying,

"Welcome home, Maisie".

She also heard

the bluebirds

and the squirrels

welcoming her to

her
new
home.

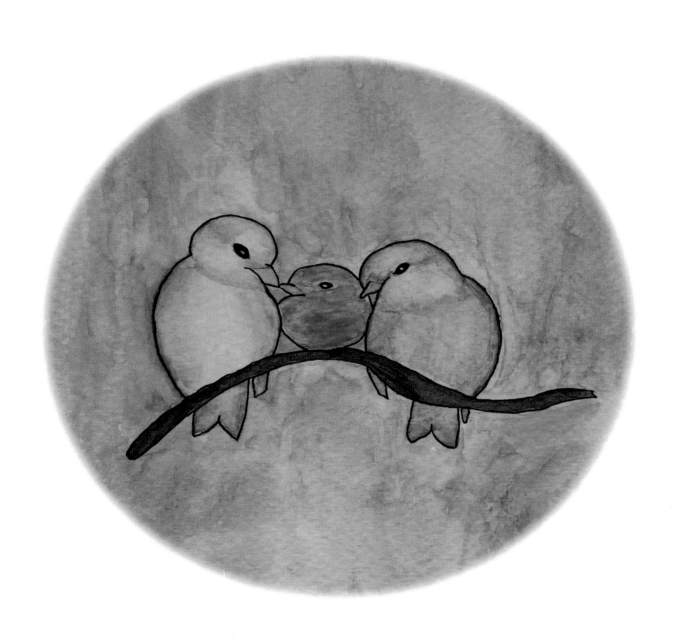

At the edge

of the clearing.

Darla said softly

"Welcome

home.

Maisie".

When they stopped

at frederick's

home.

Maisie saw all

of the other

foxes

come out from

behind the

trees

and out of

their foxholes.

"Welcome
home,
Maisie!"

they all said happily.

Made in the USA
Las Vegas, NV
04 March 2022

45012683R00029